TROLL
COUNTRY

TROLL COUNTRY

by Edward Marshall
pictures by James Marshall

THE DIAL PRESS · NEW YORK

Published by
The Dial Press
1 Dag Hammarskjold Plaza
New York, New York 10017

Library of Congress Cataloging in Publication Data
Marshall, Edward. Troll country.
Summary: Elsie Fay ventures into the deep, dark woods,
meets a troll, and attempts to outsmart him.
[1. Trolls—Fiction]
I. Marshall, James, 1942–   II. Title.
PZ7.M35655Tr   [E]   79-19324
ISBN 0-8037-6211-9 lib. bdg.   ISBN 0-8037-6210-0 pbk.

The art for each picture consists of a black
ink line-drawing with three overlays prepared
in pencil and reproduced in gray, green, and rust.

For Susan Korn Blutter
and
William Gray

"Elsie!

Elsie Fay!

Elsie Fay Johnson!"

Mrs. Johnson was calling

Elsie Fay.

"That child is never around

when I need her."

Mrs. Johnson tried again.

"Elsie Fay, where are you?"

she called.

"I am getting cross!"

"Oh, fudge," said Elsie Fay.

"I want to read.

But I don't want Mama to get cross."

She stopped reading

and went inside.

"Where were you, dear?"

asked Mrs. Johnson.

"I want you to go to market."

"I was reading," said Elsie Fay.

"I was reading about trolls."

"I once met a troll,"

said Elsie's mother.

"Did you?" cried Elsie Fay.

"Tell me, tell me, oh, please."

"Well," said her mother,

"when I was a little girl—"

"Oh, no," said Mr. Johnson,

"not that old story again."

"Hush," said his wife.

"It is very interesting."

"Go on," said Elsie Fay.

Mrs. Johnson began again.

"When I was a little girl," she said,

"I once took a shortcut home

through the deep, dark woods."

"Oooh," said Elsie Fay.

"And just as I was coming

to a little bridge,"

said Mrs. Johnson,

"I saw someone."

Elsie Fay was all ears.

"Who was it?" she asked.

"An odd little man,"
said her mother.
"He was very clumsy,
and he smelled very, very bad."

"That was a troll!" cried Elsie Fay.

"Nonsense," said Mr. Johnson.

"That was probably old Pop Hansen,
who cut wood. He was all thumbs,
and he never took a bath
in his life."

"No," said Mrs. Johnson.

"It was someone else.

Someone with mean little eyes."

"That was a troll," said Elsie Fay.

Mrs. Johnson went on.

"He was peeking out
from under the bridge," she said.

"Trolls live under bridges,"
said Elsie Fay.

"It says so in my book."

"There are no trolls,"
said Mr. Johnson firmly.

"If that is so," said his wife,
"why do they call that part
of the woods Troll Country?"

"It is just a name,"
said Mr. Johnson. "Just a name."

"Tell me more," said Elsie Fay.
"Did the troll have
a short temper and a long tail?"

"Yes, he did," said her mother.
"And great big ears and messy hair."

Mr. Johnson put down his paper.

"They say that trolls
are very greedy," he said.
"They say that trolls
break their word and tell lies."
"I thought you said
there are no trolls," said his wife.
"That is true," said Mr. Johnson.

"It also says in my book
that trolls like to play tricks,"
said Elsie Fay.
"Oh my, yes," said her mother.
"Trolls love to trick people.
But they are not very good at it.
Trolls are *not* smart."
"Did the troll try to trick you?"
asked Elsie Fay.

"I beat him to it," said her mother.

"But I had to think fast."

Elsie Fay sat on the edge of her seat.

"There was no time to get away,"

said Mrs. Johnson.

"So I knew I had to be clever."

"What did you do?" asked Elsie Fay.

"I asked the troll where I could find

the smartest troll in the woods,"

said her mother.

"All trolls *think* they are smart."

"And what did the troll say?"

asked Elsie Fay.

"He told me that I was looking at
the smartest troll in the woods,"
said Mrs. Johnson.
"I said that I did not believe him,
and he became very angry.
He jumped up and down,
and he bit his tail."

"What did you do?" asked Elsie Fay.
Mrs. Johnson smiled and said,
"I opened my purse. I took out
a tiny mirror and I gave it to him.

He had never seen a mirror before.
I told him that he was looking at
a picture of the smartest troll
in the woods."

"What did the troll do then?"
asked Elsie Fay.
"He looked very carefully
at the mirror," said Mrs. Johnson.

"And he became even angrier.
He wanted to know where he
could find that smart troll."

Elsie Fay was too excited to speak.

Mrs. Johnson went on.

"I told him," she said,

"that the smart troll in the picture

lived on the other side

of the deep, dark woods."

"And?" said Mr. Johnson.

"And," said his wife,

"he hurried away

to have a look for himself."

"Your mother is very clever,"
said Mr. Johnson to Elsie Fay.
Elsie Fay smiled.

"Oh, Mother," said Elsie Fay.

"If I ever meet a troll,

I will be clever too."

"I hope so," said her mother.

"And now it is time for you

to go to market."

"Oh, yes," said Elsie Fay.

Mrs. Johnson gave Elsie Fay

a large basket and a long list.

"Be sure not to forget

the sweet rolls," she said.

"I won't," said Elsie Fay.

When Elsie Fay got to the market,
she gave the grocer her list.
"Please don't forget the sweet trolls,"
she said. "I mean sweet rolls."

On the way home Elsie Fay passed
the deep, dark woods.

"Maybe I will meet a troll,"
she said.

Elsie Fay went into the woods.
In no time she found herself
in a deep, dark place.

"This is very, very spooky,"
she said to herself.

Up ahead she saw a small bridge.

"Hmm," she said.

"Trolls live under bridges."

But Elsie Fay did not turn back.

She came to the bridge

and she listened carefully.

There was not a sound.

Elsie Fay stepped onto the bridge.

All of a sudden,

out from under the bridge,

came an odd little man.

He had a long tail.

He had mean little eyes.

He smelled bad.

And he did not look smart.

Elsie Fay knew he was a troll.

"Grr," he said.

Elsie Fay was worried.

"I should not be here,"

she thought.

"Grr," said the troll.

He came closer.

Elsie Fay began to tremble.

The troll smacked his lips

and rubbed his ugly little hands

together.

Elsie Fay had to think fast.

"Good afternoon," she said.

"My name is Elsie Fay.

I am looking for the smartest troll

in the woods."

"Ha!" said the troll.

"I have heard *that* before!"

"Oh, dear," thought Elsie Fay.

She knew she had to think faster.

"Well, in that case," she said

to him,

"any troll will do."

"I am a troll," he said.

"Oh, but you are not a troll,"

said Elsie Fay.

The troll stood still.

He scratched his chin.

"Yes, I am," he said.

"Of course I am."

"No," said Elsie Fay loudly.

"Yes!" said the troll even louder.

"And why do you think
you are a troll?"
said Elsie Fay.
"Well, for one thing,
I have a long tail," said the troll.

"Cats and rats have long tails,"
said Elsie Fay.
The troll did not like *that*!

"I have very big ears," said the troll,
feeling his ears.

"That is nothing," said Elsie Fay.

"My Uncle Billy has very big ears,
and he is not a troll."

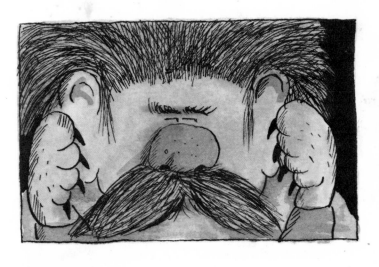

"I smell bad," said the troll.

Elsie Fay told a fib.

"You smell fresh and sweet," she said.

The troll was now confused.

"But, but," he said.

He tried to think fast.

Suddenly he had an idea.

"I am mean!" he yelled.

"Fudge and fiddlesticks,"
said Elsie Fay. "Anybody can be mean.
No, you are not a troll."

The troll was most upset.

He jumped up and down.

He bit his tail.

He kicked an old tree stump

and hurt his ugly foot.

"Ouch!" he yelled.

"Of course," said Elsie Fay,

"there is only one way to prove

you really *are* a troll."

"Oh, yes?" said the troll.

"Trolls are very graceful,"

said Elsie Fay.

"Quite true," said the troll,

tripping over his tail.

"And I have heard that trolls
can even stand on their heads,"
said Elsie Fay.
The troll had never stood on his head,
but he did not want to say so.
"I can stand on my head," he lied.
"I do it all the time."
"Show me," said Elsie Fay.

"I don't have to if I don't want to,"
said the troll.

"I knew it," said Elsie Fay.
"You are *not* a troll."
Now the troll was hopping mad.
"I'll show you!" he cried.
The troll bent over.
He put his hands on the ground.

"I am watching," said Elsie Fay.

The troll tried to put his legs

in the air.

A tiny mirror fell out of his pocket.

Elsie Fay picked it up.

"Here I go," said the troll.

With a loud thud
the troll fell over.

"Ooops," he said.

"Ah-ha," said Elsie Fay.

"I am out of shape,"

said the troll.

"I shall get it this time."

And this time too he fell over.

"One more time," he said.

And he fell over again.

"Just once more," he said.

"Easy does it."

This time he did not lose his balance.

"Tra-la!" he sang.

The troll was standing on his head!

"You see!" he cried.

"I really am a troll!"

But there was no one

to answer him.

Elsie Fay was on her way home.

Mrs. Johnson was waiting for her.

"I was worried," she said.

"I had such an exciting adventure,"
said Elsie Fay. "I met a troll!"

"Where did you meet him?"
asked her mother.

"On the bridge in the deep, dark woods," said Elsie Fay. "Did the troll have a long tail, a short temper, and messy hair?" asked her mother.

"Yes," said Elsie Fay, "and he smelled very, very bad."

"That was indeed a troll," said her mother.

"Nonsense," said Mr. Johnson.

"My, my," said Mrs. Johnson,
reaching into the market basket.
"What is this?"

Elsie Fay was ashamed.

"Oh, dear," she said. "I forgot
to give the troll his mirror."

"Don't worry," said her mother.

"It did not belong to him
in the first place.
It belongs to me."

"Trolls, trolls," said Mr. Johnson.

"There *are* no trolls.
And that is that."